For my daughter Tahlia, four,
and my grandmother Anyu, ninety-four:
Thank you for your ageless inspiration.—V. M.

Copyright © 2004 by NordSüd Verlag AG, Gossau Zürich, Switzerland
First published in Switzerland under the title *Warum so schüchtern?*
English translation copyright © 2005 by North-South Books Inc., New York

First published in the United States, Great Britain, Canada, Australia, and New Zealand in 2005
by North-South Books, an imprint of NordSüd Verlag AG, Gossau Zürich, Switzerland.
Distributed in the United States by North-South Books Inc., New York.

Library of Congress Cataloging-in-Publication Data is available.
A CIP catalogue record for this book is available from The British Library.
ISBN 0-7358-1967-X (trade edition)
1 3 5 7 9 HC 10 8 6 4 2
ISBN 0-7358-1968-8 (library edition)
1 3 5 7 9 LE 10 8 6 4 2
Printed in Denmark

For more information about our books, and the authors and artists
who create them, visit our web site: www.northsouth.com

So Shy

By Vicki Morrison

Illustrated by Nora Hilb

North-South Books

New York · London

Jake sat alone on the beach. There were lots of children playing on the sand, but Jake sat there all alone.

Jake was shy. He watched the other children playing and longed to join them, but he was afraid to ask.

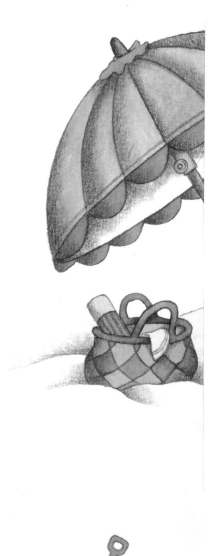

Sometimes Jake pretended that his shadow was his best friend. He wasn't shy at all with his shadow.

Everywhere that Jake went, so did his shadow. They played on the beach together, running through the waves that crashed along the shore. They built their own sandcastle, with walls so high that nobody could get inside, except, of course, Jake and his shadow.

But shadows can't talk, so Jake never laughed or joked with his best friend.

"You're the only friend I've got," said Jake sadly. He held out his hand and tried to touch his shadow. "You're great, but I wish I could have a *real* friend, one who could talk to me. I just need to be brave enough to find one."

His shadow nodded.

Jake and his shadow walked to the playground. Jake
stood on the path and watched the other children racing
around, having fun. He really wanted to join them, but he
was just too shy to ask.

Jake spotted the swings. "Do you want to ride on those
swings?" he asked his shadow.

His shadow nodded and moved quickly toward the
swings, pulling Jake behind him. Together, they flew high
in the air.

"That was fun," said Jake, hopping off the swing. "Do you want to play on the rocks now?"

His shadow nodded and, with Jake by his side, jumped from rock to rock all along the shore.

Jake thought he'd try something harder. "Do you
want to climb that big tree and hang on like monkeys?"
he asked his shadow.

His shadow nodded. Together, they slowly climbed
up the branches, all the way to the top. And carefully
his shadow helped Jake back down to the ground.

Jake and his shadow sat quietly beneath the tree. "You're a great friend," he told his shadow. "You can swing and jump and climb." Jake sighed. "If only you could talk."

His shadow nodded.

Suddenly Jake heard someone crying. He turned, and there stood a little girl.

"What's wrong?" asked Jake. He was so concerned about the little girl that he forgot for a moment that he was shy.

"My cat is up in that tree," said the girl. "She can't get down, and I'm too scared to climb up."

Jake wanted to help, but he wasn't sure if he could do it by himself. He turned to his shadow and whispered, "Should we try to climb the tree like we did before and get the cat?"

His shadow nodded quickly.

Jake's shadow helped him onto the first branch. Then Jake began to climb. He was thinking so hard about where to put his feet that he didn't notice that his shadow was still on the ground.

"Come here," Jake whispered to the cat. "I'm going to help you."

Jake cuddled the cat in his arms and carried her safely back down the tree. That's when he saw his shadow, waiting on the ground.

Wow! he thought. I did it all by myself!

"Oh, thank you!" cried the little girl, hugging her cat. "You were so brave to rescue her."

And Jake *did* feel brave, brave enough to ask, "What's your name?"

"Julie," the girl replied.

Jake and Julie sat beneath the tree. When Jake turned, he saw that his shadow was sitting there, too, right next to Julie's shadow.

Soon Jake and Julie were talking and laughing together—and so were their shadows. Jake liked it that Julie also had a shadow for a friend. Maybe she was a little shy, too, he thought. But he liked it even better that he and Julie were real friends.

"Come on!" cried Jake, taking Julie's hand. And as they ran back to the beach, their shadows ran behind them—four friends having a wonderful time together.